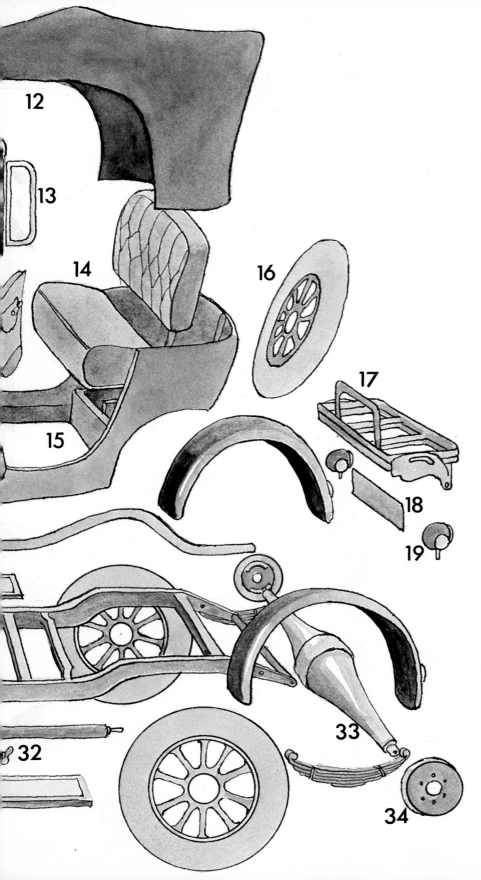

4 Bonnet
5 Engine
6 Gearbox
7 Side lamps
8 Horn
9 Windscreen
10 Mirror
11 Front seats
12 Hood
13 Folding windscreen
14 Back seats
15 Body
16 Spare wheel
17 Luggage carrier
18 Number plate
19 Tail lamps
20 Head lamps
21 Front axle
22 Springs
23 Mud-guards
24 Exhaust pipe
25 Steering column
26 Wheels
27 Petrol can
28 Petrol tank
29 Chassis
30 Propeller shaft
31 Running boards
32 Fire extinguisher
33 Back axle
34 Brake drums

For Mimi
with my love

# GUMDROP
# MAKES A START

*Story and pictures by Val Biro*

HODDER AND STOUGHTON
LONDON   SYDNEY   AUCKLAND   TORONTO

IT WAS on a sunny day in March, a very long time ago, that a young boy stood by the gates of The Austin Motor Company. He stood there most days after school to watch the new cars coming out of the factory. This young boy liked a lot of things, but he liked cars best of all in the world.

As he stood watching, he saw yet another new car being rolled into the forecourt. He opened his eyes even wider than usual, because somehow this car was different. It was blue with black wings and a brass radiator. It had a black hood and four brass lamps which sparkled in the sunshine. But what made this car so different was the curly brass horn bolted to the windscreen! This was the most beautiful Austin Clifton Heavy 12/4 that he had ever seen in his life.

'That's the car for me!'
he shouted, and the men
around the car laughed.
'Wait until you hear the
engine!' called the foreman
as he placed himself in the
driving seat. He set the levers
on the steering-wheel and pulled the
choke out. Then he pressed his foot
on the starter button. The car went 'Guuuum.'
The foreman pushed in the choke and pulled out the
ignition button and pressed his foot again. This time
the car went 'Drrrropopopop' and the engine started to run.

The boy was enchanted.
What a lovely sound!
Guuuum – Drrrropopopop.
As if the car had called
out its own name. 'That's it!'
he declared to one and all.
'That's his name. GUMDROP!'
And he felt convinced that Gumdrop
was the only car for him. He longed
to have that beautiful car for his very own.
But as he was only seven he could do nothing about it.
So he took a last lingering look and walked home in a dream.

Some weeks later Gumdrop stood sparkling among all the other
new cars in the showroom when a grand lady sailed in. 'I am the
Lady Mayoress,' she announced, 'and I want a car in which I
shall look my best.' She inspected each car in turn and then
stopped in front of Gumdrop.

'Look at this, now,' she cried. 'What a magnificent motor! And it matches my dress to perfection!' So she bought Gumdrop on the spot and was driven home in splendour.

Later that year, on the day of the Procession, the Lord Mayor and his Lady looked at their best. People cheered as they saw them waving graciously from the back seat of Gumdrop. The Lord Mayor's Lady felt a little peeved because she thought that there were more cheers for Gumdrop than for her. This made her wave even more graciously.

Soon it started to rain.
'My new hat!' screamed the Lady.
'It will be ruined!' So the chauffeur
stopped Gumdrop to put the hood up. But by the
time he managed to fix it the Lady's hat was in a mess.
She was furious: so furious that she decided to sell Gumdrop
and buy a saloon-car instead. It would at least keep her hats dry.

So Gumdrop was for sale again. There he stood among all the other second-hand cars for a long time until, one day, a small car drew up. Mr and Mrs Septimus Bunch got out, followed by their five children. They were looking for a bigger car with enough room for the whole family.

'Look at that!' they cried when they saw Gumdrop. There was certainly enough room for them all and they always wanted an Austin 12/4. What is more, there was even a folding windscreen for the back! So Mr Bunch bought Gumdrop on the spot.

Gumdrop was kept very busy by the Bunches.

He took the children to school,

he took Mrs Bunch to the shops

and he took Mr Bunch to town.

Best of all, he took the whole family on holidays.

They drove up steep mountains,      They picnicked in shady woods

and they went down to the sea. Gumdrop spent many happy years with the
family, while the children grew bigger and bigger. Soon they could
hardly squeeze into Gumdrop any more.
And when they did, they had to get
out and push every time Gumdrop
came to a hill, because they
were too heavy for him.

So in the end Mr Bunch sadly decided to sell Gumdrop and get
an even bigger car for his family.

The man who bought Gumdrop this time was Freddy Bracegirdle. He was a fireman and he drove Gumdrop to the Fire Station each morning. One day, when all the big fire engines were out, there was yet another fire-call. 'We have no engines left!' cried the Station Commander. 'What shall we do?' Freddy had an idea. 'Let's hitch the trailer-pump to my car and go to the fire like that!'

And there went Gumdrop, with the firemen inside, a ladder on his hood and the pump trailing behind and Freddy honking the horn all the time. Gumdrop got them to the fire in no time and the firemen soon put it out.

'You have done very well,' said the Station Commander when they got back. 'In fact this car seems to be made for the job. So we shall use it from now on as an Auxiliary Fire Engine.' He patted Gumdrop on the bonnet which was all covered in soot and grime. The boy at the factory gates would hardly have recognised his sparkling new car by now, but he would have felt very proud of it.

So Gumdrop became a very special fire engine. He was the only blue one in the whole town and people cheered when they saw him flash by with the pump trailing behind and his horn honking away.

He was always first to arrive
at the fire. His pump was unhitched
and ready in no time, and Gumdrop stood
bravely by as the firemen fought the flames.

He spent some exciting years as a fire engine and had many
adventures. But the time came when the Station acquired some
new ones and there was no more work for him. Freddy had
another car by then anyway, so he sadly decided to sell
Gumdrop. The firemen took a fond farewell of him and the
Station Commander gave Gumdrop a special badge to thank
him for his long and brave service with them.

Gumdrop was quite an old car by now and somewhat battered. People called him 'the old crock', or 'the old banger', or just 'the heap'. It was most unkind of them. In fact Mr Peabody Parsnip was rather annoyed when he heard these names, because he was Gumdrop's new owner. He was a greengrocer and he used Gumdrop for his deliveries.

His customers weren't too pleased either when they saw such an old car at their smart front doors. This worried Mr Parsnip a lot because he had a reputation to think of. So when he managed to buy a new delivery van a year or two later, he sold Gumdrop to his neighbour, Farmer Clodbury.

Gumdrop had to work hard at the farm.

Farmer Clodbury would drive him to market
and return with boxes and sacks
piled high on the back seat.

Gumdrop would fetch the hay in
from the field, and carry timber for the fences.

On Saturdays young Giles
Clodbury would climb into
Gumdrop and give himself
a few driving lessons
round the meadow.

Poor old Gumdrop was getting more and more
battered as time wore on, until one day
Farmer Clodbury drove him into a
barn and left him there. He
had no further use for
such an old car.

But the hens thought that Gumdrop would make an excellent nest
and they moved in to lay their eggs on the comfortable seats. And
there they remained, scratching and clucking contentedly, while
Gumdrop sagged more and more and began to rust slowly away.

One day a man drove his truck into the farmyard. Charlie Mead was a scrap-merchant and he was looking for old bits of metal to buy. 'There's nothing much around here,' said Farmer Clodbury, when Charlie noticed Gumdrop in the barn.

'What about that old heap over there?' he asked. The farmer scratched his head. 'I would be sorry to part with that car because it's been useful in the past,' he said. 'But you can take if you must, because times are hard and I need the money.'

So Charlie paid the farmer and hitched Gumdrop to his truck. 'You must have been quite a smart car once,' he told Gumdrop as he drove away, 'but nobody wants an old banger like you any more. So off you go to the car-breakers tomorrow.'

Early next morning a man came into the scrapyard and looked
around. When he saw Gumdrop he stopped, and stared.
'Why,' he said, 'that's an Austin Clifton Heavy Twelve
Four, and it must surely be blue under all that dirt!
And look, there's the brass horn still fixed to the windscreen!'
He turned excitedly to Charlie. 'I will buy this car,' he said,
'because I think it is the one I remember seeing when I
was a small boy.'

   He remembered sure enough, because all those years ago it
was he who used to stand at the factory gates. And now he
was none other than Mr Josiah Oldcastle, and he has been
dreaming about Gumdrop ever since!

'Just one thing,' he said. 'I would like to try the engine.'
So he and Charlie fixed a new battery to the terminals and filled
Gumdrop with petrol, oil and water. Then Mr Oldcastle seated
himself in the driving seat and pressed the button.
'Guuuum,' said Gumdrop.
Mr Oldcastle pulled out the
ignition and pressed again.
'Drrrropopopop,' said Gumdrop.
'GUMDROP!' shouted
Mr Oldcastle in triumph.
'There's no doubt about it.
This is my old Gumdrop!'

He was beside himself with joy. He could hardly wait to pay
Charlie. He could hardly stop himself from dancing around as
he pumped up the tyres. Then he settled back in the driving seat
again. His dream had come true and Gumdrop was his at long
last. So, with a grateful wave to Charlie, Mr Oldcastle drove
Gumdrop home.